Let your sparkle shine!

Pamela Melon

For my children: Always stay true to yourselves.

-Mama

pamelamelon.books@gmail.com

The Face Painter's
MIRROR

by Pamela Melon

"There it is! Let's get our faces painted. I want to be a *magical* rainbow unicorn!" Ryder beamed.

"I want to be a T-Rex," Amber stomped,

"ROAR!"

Ryder asked the face painter, "could I be a rainbow unicorn please?"

"How about I give you a surprise instead?" Said the woman.

"Hmm," Ryder sighed. "I guess I like surprises."

When the face painter was done, she guided Ryder to the mirror.

POOF!

Ryder looked at himself and frowned,

"I'm a shark?"

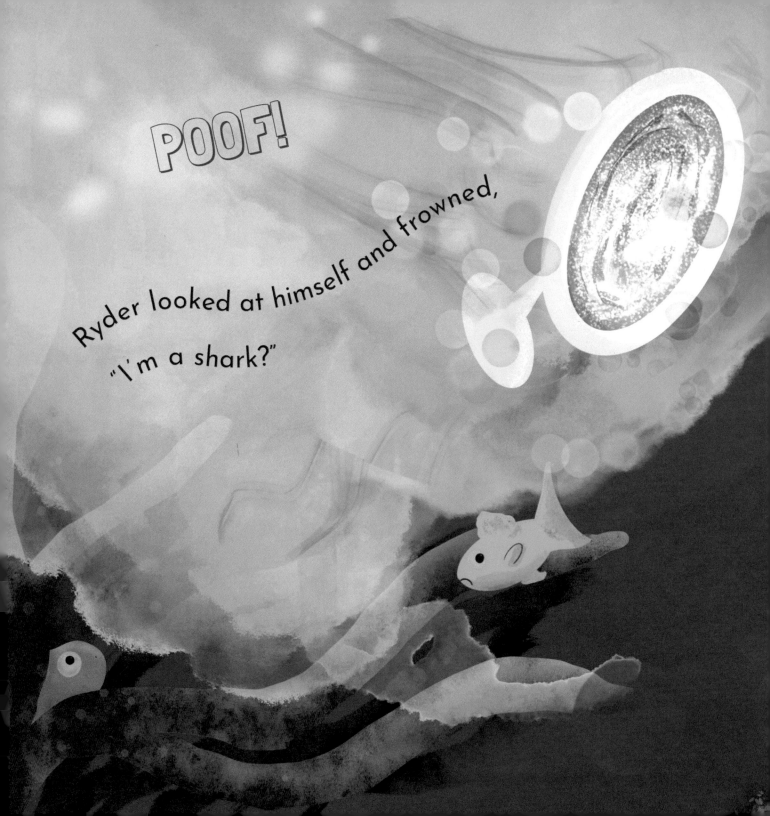

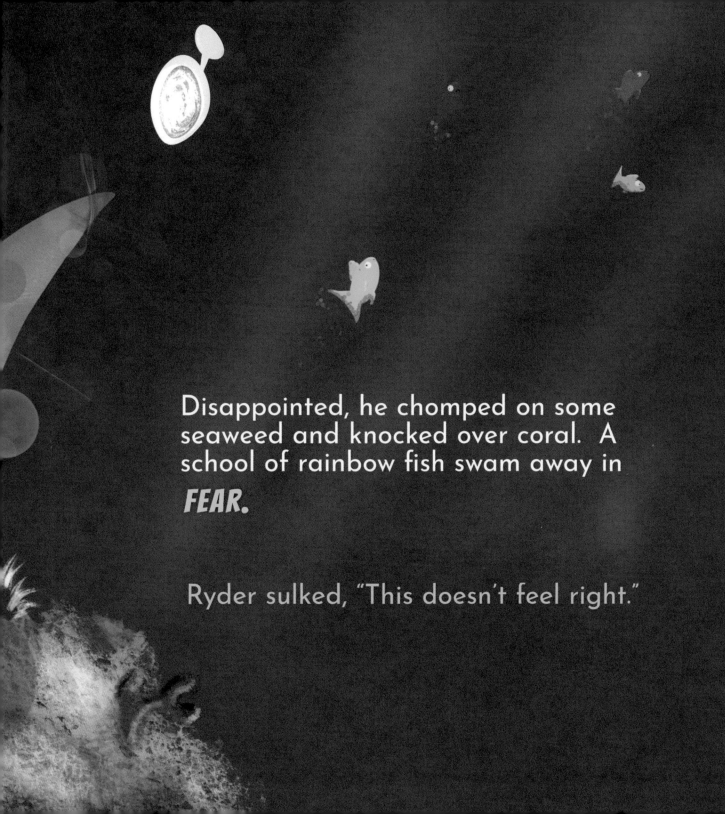

Disappointed, he chomped on some seaweed and knocked over coral. A school of rainbow fish swam away in *FEAR.*

Ryder sulked, "This doesn't feel right."

Ryder looked up at the surface and
saw a butterfly in the sky.
"Is that you, Amber?"

"It's me! That face painter
turned me into this,"
she fluttered.

"Didn't you ask for a T-Rex?"
Ryder asked, "Why couldn't we get
what we asked for. We can't even
play together now."

A few drops of
the angry ocean
leaked out
of his
eyes

"Let's wash this off and try again, Ryder," said Amber.

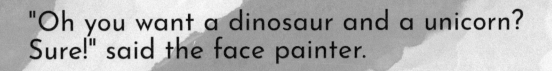

"Oh you want a dinosaur and a unicorn? Sure!" said the face painter.

"This time she gets it!" Ryder smiled.

"I'm ready to see my unicorn face!" Ryder pranced.

"WOAH!"
CRASH!

Ryder's large feet got in the way.

"Ryder, what happened?" Amber asked.

"I tried to dance but my big claws got in the way!" cried Ryder.

"Well, I wish I had those big feet so I could stomp! These hooves aren't heavy enough. See?" Amber's hooves tapped the ground.

"She got it backwards again," complained Ryder.

Ryder turned towards the face painter, "NO! This is all wrong! I wanted to be the unicorn and SHE wanted to be the T-Rex. Why won't you let us choose?"

She thought about it.

And then she remembered being told she could not like something.

"OK. You two are right. It is your choice. I paint faces to make children happy. Will it make you happy?"

"YES!" Exclaimed the two.

"Well let's get started!" the woman responded.

Ryder tried not to smile and sat as still as a statue.

The paintbrush swirled cold paint on his cheek.

Next he picked out some glitter to make his face and heart sparkle.

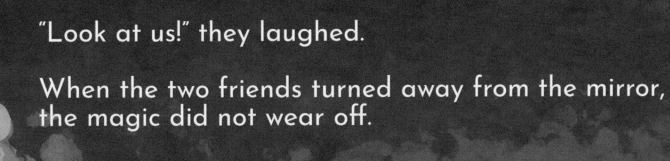

"Look at us!" they laughed.

When the two friends turned away from the mirror, the magic did not wear off.

for more please visit:
www.pamelamelon.wixsite.com/books
instagram: @pamela.melon

Pamela Melon is a mom of two and early childhood educator from British Columbia. She is the daughter of South Americans and grew up living there as well as B.C.

She was inspired to write this story when her five year old son was so excited to get a rainbow unicorn painted on his face, and the face painter gave him a shark instead.

He got his unicorn the next time.

Made in the USA
Columbia, SC
12 October 2021